Jim Friedlander

Illustrated by

Anthony DeVito

The Wall

Copyright © 2017 by James Friedlander

Paperback
ISBN-13   978-1-5471961-2-8
ISBN   1-547196-1-2-2

Printed in the United States of America

Characters in The Wall:

Bugle Beagle-	Detective Molly hires to find the rabbits
Mr. Donkey (Wonkey) -	Producer at *What We need to Know*
Garland Gila-	Gilda's husband and a reporter for *La Verdad*
Gilda Gila-	She sees the rabbits while they are lost and circling and tells her husband.
Henry Hedgehog-	Stringer for *Euroblab*
Hillary Harrishawk-	Bugle's research assistant
Marty Moose-	Presidential Candidate for the Carnivore Party
Melba Mockingbird-	Mr. Donkey's secretary
Molly Mallard-	Senior reporter for *What We Need to Know*
Millie Millipede-	Head of border security
Ms. Peggy Pigchops-	Anchor at What We Need to Know
Phineus Fox-	Press secretary to the president
Rabbit Family:	Rufus- the grandfather
	June- the grandmother
	Jeremiah-the father
	Jenny- the mother
	Julie- a few months old
	Jessie- the brother
Ronnie Roadrunner-	Marty's chief of staff
Simon Salamander-	Tech at *What We Need to Know*
Tamara Tamarin-	Tommy's girlfriend
Tobias Toad-	Molly's friend from Central Animalia and a reporter
Tommy Tamarin-	President of Animalia

Chapter 1

A cacophony of verbiage and beautiful faces vibrated on the thirty monitors, end to end, staring back at Mr. Donkey, delivering an indecipherable report of the day's events. Mr. Donkey, the head producer for *Everything We Need to Know*, the nightly news, watched them full of rehearsed sincerity. He consumed all simultaneously, regurgitating something palatable for the TV viewer. It was up to Donkey to switch from monitor to monitor to decide what was worthy of being called breaking news, human interest, and background. He sat in his office chair twitching his long brown tail nervously as if swatting flies, huge eyes glued on the screens, waiting for something to catch his attention, something he thought would hook viewers during the next broadcast. His jaw traveled at a rate of speed appropriate to his thought process while keeping a cud going. Only when he had made a decision would the cud be allowed to slide down, lubricating his dry throat.

On the floor below, lines from various reporters in the field fed the main frame computer storing thousands of stories arriving every day to be organized and prioritized. Once entered, they were scanned for serious irregularities, and if none were found, stored as "TRUTH". Simon Salamander, the technician for all this hardware, lived on this floor and only left once a year when he was forced to take his vacation. During that time, he went to an apartment he kept so he could say he had a home. He thought if he did not have a home address he would be considered homeless. He paid for it to be cleaned once a month. All bills were on automatic payment. He compared it to the perpetual care he bought for his mother's cemetery plot. It was the part of his life that he wished simply did not exist. Simon even found a food service that would stock his refrigerator ahead of his forced exile so he did not have to concern himself with going to a store to buy groceries, a waste of time.

When a screen went blank or the image flipped upside down or zoomed in or out for no particular reason that anyone else could understand, he was the designated expert. As the hardware had become capable of doing more, the problems had multiplied. It seemed that as soon as he fixed a piece of software, an automatic upgrade of new, more sophisticated software was automatically downloaded. It kept him busy. When he returned from the two weeks in his apartment, it often took him several months to catch up with the problems. His fill-in, who was usually from a temp agency and not familiar with the routine, caused more problems than solutions. Part of his vacation he did appreciate was being away from Mr. Donkey or "Wonkey" as he called him. It annoyed him that everyone referred to him as "the tech", with little appreciation for his part in the broadcast. He was in the shadows. Even so, he watched "What" every night to observe choices Wonkey made. When asked if he watched he would reply, "only to check the quality of the image."

The face that dominated the news program was Ms. Piggie Pigchops, the anchor and public face of the news. Simon wondered what qualified her for the job. There were rumors that floated around the lunch room about her and Wonkey but who had started them and their veracity were a question. How much was jealousy? Probably a good deal. It was the story that all the reporters were very interested in breaking but didn't have the balls to pursue. And somehow she had managed to hold the job for twelve years, all the time keeping her face and figure with the help of modern surgery. When her jowls required a tweak or her hide a tuck an inch or two, she would suddenly go away to an exotic land for vacation and come back having lost ten years.

Simon enjoyed the thinking if she wasn't careful she might lose too many years and end up a piglet again.

She did her best to interpret the news so the audience would not be confused. A practiced viewer could tell how Ms. Pigchops felt about a story by observing her ears, which at rest lay flat in a horizontal position. When she wanted to impart a sense of sadness, such as a mass shooting, she would let her ears droop. When her ears were straight up the viewer was in for a shock. This was reserved for celebrity or political scandals. For special interest events that might bore the watcher, she flared the nostrils on her perfectly round snout. The audience couldn't help but pay attention as their diameter expanded and contracted. If anyone could have seen the bucket she kept under her stool and watched the curly tail as she lifted it to let go a warm pile of poo, they would have understood her true feelings.

Simon felt totally disengaged from Ms. Pigchops even though they were each important in their own way. She depended on him but lived in a world under the lights of stardom. How was it fair that the two were mutually exclusive. As long as all the feeds made it to Wonkey for his perusal, Simon had filled his role. The work was never finished so his obligation went unfulfilled. In fact, he was in a constant state of agitation. This agitation kept him so occupied that there was little time to think about Pigchops or any other "diversions" as he called them.

Mr. Donkey had figured out Simon long ago and took full advantage of his agitation. He asked questions that Simon did not have time for, such as, "have you tested that new program that was written up in the *News Journal?*" This kept Simon off balance, always thinking that he should be doing more. As Wonkey controlled what made it to Ms. Pigchop's desk to read each evening, he thought of himself as the big cheese. When asked to speak at journalism conferences, he was sure to never mention the other members of the news crew, leaving novices to believe that he was it. When young journalists flocked about him like birds to a feeder, he dispensed tidbits of wisdom filled with famous names so that there was no mistaking who the real star of the show was.

The Wall

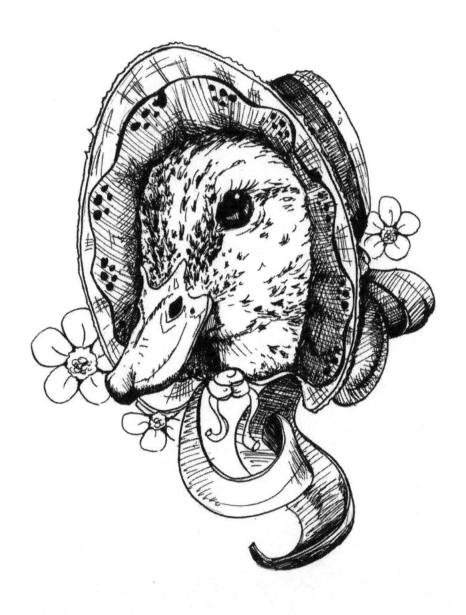

Chapter 2

During the summer, when the government was on vacation so there was no daily flow of releases to fill the time, Donkey's job became much harder. The president might be off in some foreign land involved in peace talks or trying to put together a trade agreement, but these made for a very dull newscast. The producers of the game show that followed had leaned on him to make sure that he did not lose any audience during his show. There was fifteen minutes of Ms Pigchop's news to fill and it must hold the audience's attention. When Wonkey felt the heat from the producers, he made sure Pigchops felt it also. She knew she had not been chosen for her analysis and insight alone. She had to be someone that the females could admire for her good taste in clothing and the males cold enjoy watching. It was a balancing act. Too much sex appeal and the females might be offended. Not enough and the males would wander to the refrigerator. Clothes designers were constantly approaching her with their latest design. She not only was able keep the clothes but was paid to introduce them to her audience. In the back of her mind she thought if she was ever let go as the anchor, she could try to make a living modeling. However, she also knew that she would never get the same exposure she got every weekday evening in her present position. It couldn't be better.

It was during the summer that this story took place. Many of the animals of the forest, present characters excluded, were on vacation. Those not vacationing were in such a state of torpor that it was hardly worth the effort to entertain them. Anything that flickered on the screen could keep them amused.

Molly Mallard, one of the senior reporters for *Everything*, finding nothing of import to report, decided to fly south to see if her friend Tobias Toad might have a feature she could use.

Toby lived in a land thought of as "off-limits" by many of the animals of the forest, too dangerous. What exactly those dangers were they would be hard pressed to explain. Bad behavior was a typical answer and seemed to suffice. Although no animal would ever say this, they spoke a different language and believed in a different creation story from the one northern animals grew up with. Theirs explained how the first animal was conceived in the image of a many tailed god and was sacrificed only to be resurrected as a mosquito. Anyway, Toby and Molly met at the University of Wisdom where they had been in the same language class. Molly was very open minded when it came to class consciousness and wanted to be able to communicate with the workers when she migrated during the winter months. She looked forward to speaking with them while she went to get grain. And, given her very bad sense of direction, she was always stopping to ask one which way was El Norte. Toby had needed an easy course to bring up his grade point average and, since the class was to learn his native language he felt he couldn't miss. Toby liked Molly as soon as he met her and offered to help her with her homework. She, being a slow learner who rarely stopped quacking long enough to listen to the teacher during class, was glad to accept. After class they would go to a pond in a nearby park where Molly would swim about and Toby would hop onto a lily pad near the shore. He did not like water, being a toad, but put up with it since it made Molly feel comfortable. She swam back and forth as he conjugated the lesson's verbs and had her repeat them.

Molly made her travel plans and called Toby to tell him when she would arrive. Toby asked if she would like to go on a picnic that Sunday. It would be just like their student days. He had in mind the pond where they used to practice their language lessons. Now they could just relax and not be bothered with trying to concentrate on homework. She thought that was a splendid idea. Most of the other mallards were already heading north so she would be on her own when Toby was busy with his job at the paper. She could spend the rest of the week roaming from pond to pond looking for another duck to quack at, a black duck, merganser, wood, shoveler, any kind. By the time the weekend came, she would be excited to have some company.

Toby found some nice dragonflies and wrapped them in a damp leaf to keep them fresh. He took a quick splash in a puddle to rinse off the dust and put on his vest and bowler hat. Checking his reflection in a puddle and tipping his hat slightly to give himself a more jaunty appearance, he decided he looked quite dapper. He felt that toads were not always given the respect they were due and wanted to be sure Molly did not feel that way. She was an important individual, after all, seen on television by millions. Her name was a household word. It was a privilege to know her as a friend. He could tell the other toads that he was a friend of the famous Molly Mallard. And today he hoped to put her in his debt. He had something important to tell her.

Toads are a bit reclusive and are not usually part of the mainstream, so social trends are not their forte, but Toby was beginning to think he would like to be more respected in his community. He believed his friendship with Molly was a way to improve that standing.

They met in the early morning as the sun was just beginning to show its face, the soft light filtered by ground fog through the ferns. She had chosen to wear a bonnet covered in flowers with a chin strap, to keep it secured while she was in flight. Toby thought it framed her face in a most lovely way and told her so. They spread out the blanket, which she brought, and opened their lunches. She slurped her seaweed as delicately as one can slurp seaweed. He chewed the head off his dragonfly, choosing a moment when she wasn't watching for fear that she might find it offensive.

15

After they finished eating they reposed and passed the time discussing the language class and the professor whom they both found a bit monotonous. Molly said she often played "Ducks in a Pond" on her cell, and Toby told her he sat next to the window so he could look for flies that gathered there. He asked her if she had a flight plan, to which she replied, she would be leaving in a week or so. The government was coming back into session and she needed to be there for the opening. He queried her about what important bills she expected to see come to the floor this session. She told him she expected it to be more of the same, animal crossing signs, territorial disputes, storm related bills, nothing to get the juices flowing. He asked her if she had heard about the jackrabbit problem. She didn't even know what a jackrabbit was except for references to them in cartoons, which she found offensive because they were based on stereotypes. She asked him to explain. Toby said he didn't have all the facts but there seemed to be a food issue for many of the indigenous rabbits, and some were reported to be heading north to her country. Exactly where they were or how many was not known but usually they traveled in vast numbers and left a scorched earth behind them. At least that's what he had heard somewhere.

The Wall

Chapter 3

At 6 AM, in a burrow not too far from the news station, the lights were beginning to come on. This hole was not just any hole. It had many grand entrances. Each one had a sign stating its intended use. One was for the representatives of the government. Others were for services such as janitorial, food, plumbers, and electricians. Staff to the representatives had their own as did the media people. The tunnels were a maze in which newbies were constantly getting lost. Fortunately there was an app for their phones to tell them where they were. Animals of every type hurried along on their errands disregarding the others. Each had a mission and time was of the essence. Over the burrow flew the flag with a single blade of grass on a field of orange. No one could remember what it represented but it was a common topic of speculation. It was seen at every public function, there to remind one and all that they belonged.

At nine o'clock the doors to the media room opened and reporters filed in for the press secretary's morning briefing. The secretary, who was perfectly groomed and perhaps a bit too fit for a badger, moved to the podium. He could have easily landed a job on a soap opera if he had not decided politics had more opportunities.

He began, "Today there will be a bill brought up that you have all been hearing about, the corn subsidy bill, number 158932-5. This bill guarantees a minimum price per bushel to corn farmers who now have to deal with fluctuating prices that put them in jeopardy of bankruptcy. The chickens and hogs all support the bill, but sheep, goats and horses are opposed."

"The next thing on the agenda is the pastures bill,

number 158932-6. This bill calls for more land being set aside for open grazing. This bill is supported by the sheep, goats, and horses but is opposed by the chickens and hogs."

"I have a handout which will give you all the particulars of these two bills. Also, the president will be completing his trip to Latinia today and will be here tomorrow to take questions on his trip. If you have any now, I will be glad to try to answer them." He pointed to a reporter near the back. "Yes, Mr. Fox."

Mr. Fox was one of the veteran capitol reporters who had a reputation for asking hard-hitting questions. "Does anyone have an idea how many kernels of corn the average chicken eats each day?'

"I'll have to get back to you on that," said the press secretary.

"Are there any other questions?"

Tony Tarantula raised one of his furry legs.

The secretary, who was a bit of an arachnophobe, tried to ignore him but he raised several more legs and was waving them about in such a way that he had everyone's attention. "Mr Secretary, how will the other animals benefit from any of these bills? They have to pay for them whether or not they eat corn or grass."

The secretary paused, then said, "I understand your concern but doesn't corn attract insects that other animals eat? Doesn't grass supply a hiding place for those insects?" The secretary was chosen for this job for a good reason.

He was getting ready to leave when Molly Mallard raised her wing.

"Yes, Molly."

"Sir, has the president mentioned the jackrabbit problem?"

The Wall

The secretary stood staring at her as if she had dropped a rock on his foot. "I am not sure I understand the question or am familiar with the circumstances. Is there a problem with jackrabbits not getting enough to eat? At this point I don't know of any bunny issues."

"It may be just a rumor sir," she said. "There may have been some sightings of large numbers of black tailed jackrabbits headed this way across the southern desert."

"I will be glad to check with Homeland Insecurity to see if they have anything. Thank you. That will be all for today."

Molly was not going to be put off that easily. "What if there is such a thing happening?"

The secretary, beginning to get annoyed said, "Molly, as I said, I will ask."

With that he turned on his paws and left the stage.

Molly wondered why he would check with Homeland Insecurity and not Immigration.

Chapter 4

In a desert to the south of Animalia, in what is called Central Animalia, the land was dead still under a full moon. Cacti dotted the earth for as far as one could see and well beyond, in fact for hundreds of miles, standing like ghosts of the people who had inhabited this land a long time ago. Now and then a roadrunner zipped about looking for a nice lizard to munch on while owls glided overhead hoping to beat them to it. In this country, consuming other animals had not been outlawed as it was in the more advanced countries. Some animals sat perfectly still, only their eyes moving, scanning the surroundings and waiting. Energy needed to be conserved here in these extremes of heat and cold, eventually dinner would arrive. Others, like coyotes, could not afford to wait and traveled paths that had always guided them to shelter, water, and food. Far above, the stars travelled across the blackness on their implacable path to nowhere.

On this night, it was not coyotes that were traveling on a particular path, one that lead north across the barren land to a different country that all the world knew as the land of milk and honey. This night it was black-tailed jackrabbits, six of them. They had waited out the heat of the day and were now hopping their way to what they thought was a better life, away from being easy prey for so many other animals. It had been a harrowing trip so far, with many close calls, but they were still all alive and hopeful. Once an owl came out of nowhere and swooped down on Julie, who was only a few months old. Rufus, her grandfather, had seen it coming and managed to push her under a rock, as the talons were about to snatch her. On another occasion, Jeremiah, Julie's father, had led a coyote on a wild goose chase away from the rest of the family and gone into Buddy, the burrowing owl's hole, just as the coyote was about to grab him. They all felt the scariest thing that had happened to them was when they got lost. They had traveled for three days, going around in a great circle until they realized they had passed the same Gila monster before. In fact, when they thought about it they realized that they had passed Gilda, that was her name, perhaps fifteen or twenty times.

When Gilda went home that night she told her husband, Garland, that she had seen something very strange, very strange indeed.

As his plane, Bald Headed Eagle 1, touched down at the Capitol Airport, President Tamarin looked out the window and was disappointed to see it was raining. He thought of "cats and dogs" but put quickly put this anachronism out of his mind. He had hoped for a photo op on his return home from this important visit to a neighboring country that was critical to his own economy. He could see, in his mind's eye, stepping from the plane, his mane getting soaked and matted down until he would look like a child's toy left outside. Wouldn't the tabloids love that? This would never do. He would have to make a dash for his limo and be whisked away. Bad timing. His aides would hear about this. Why had he not been scheduled to land on a nice sunny day? Then he remembered that he was the one that had set the schedule for this trip so he could spend time with his lover, Tamara. He could hope for a little positive press from the news conference he had planned for the following day. He brought home a signed trade deal that was good news. But in the county's vast economy it would make no more than a ripple and the press never got excited about trade deals. He needed something much bigger to get headlines. His numbers were sagging and he knew he needed something that would remind people why they had elected him in the first place. What he really needed was something that would touch the public personally.

As he stepped from under the umbrella and into his limo, he saw that he would not be riding alone. Sitting on the far end of the seat was his press secretary. They drove through the capitol forest, while the secretary filled him in on the past week. Then he was dropped off at his residence in the magnificent copper beech that the founding fathers had planted hundreds of years ago. The guards let him in, past the gate, and he climbed to the canopy to find peace in his bed. But there was no peace. The secretary's report had not been a good one. His poll numbers were way down, the economy was still sliding as it had been for months, and there were pesky reports of turmoil in Central Animalia. He tossed and turned, trying to get to sleep. Over and over he went through the various problems he confronted. He had a cabinet meeting in the morning but they would only suggest more solutions, more confusion. What he really needed was a simple problem. One that he could actually fix, that would show the voters he was in charge. He needed one that showed he could improve the state of the union, not some major issue that would be cured in another term, years after he had left office. He tossed and turned, wracking his mind. He needed help.

Garland and Gilda Gila were enjoying a dinner of kangaroo mouse when she mentioned what she had seen that day. Garland, being a reporter for *La Verdad*, was always looking for a good animal interest story. His usual beat was astronomy and weather, one of the most popular parts of the paper. All the subscribers turned to that page first to plan their day or night depending on whether they were diurnal or nocturnal. After that they wanted to know if there was anything unusual going on in their neighborhood. Then the paper went into the litter box. The story Gilda told him certainly sounded unusual. The coyotes would be interested. She told him it seemed there was a never-ending trail of the rabbits heading north. There were whole families moving, not just the young males going to search for new territory. These looked like they intended to stay. Garland thought this was worth investigating so, that evening, he packed some food and set off to the area where Gilda had seen them.

He did not like travelling during the day for fear of many hawks about searching for a meal to feed their newborns. Instead he chose a night when the moon was new and the sky very dark. This would have been a wise decision except his eyesight wasn't the best. After stumbling over rocks and almost being impaled on a prickly pear, he thought he had the spot. Finding a large rock to sit on that had been warmed during the day, he waited. From time to time he thought he heard noises in the bushes, but it always turned out to be a vole or snake heading home after imbibing too much fermented cactus juice. Long into the night his eyelids began to get heavy and he dozed off. When he woke the sun was shining brightly. He realized he had been asleep for hours. Now that he could see more clearly, he went in search of the path Gilda had described, always with an eye out for predators. What he found shocked him. There in front of him was a path obviously well used in fact so well used that it was actually depressed below the level of the surrounding land. *My God*, he thought, *how many rabbits would it take to make such a path?* It was beginning to get hot but being a good reporter he thought he should investigate this route to be sure it was what he thought. He hadn't gone far when he came to something that convinced him. There, on the side of the road, was a dead jackrabbit. It looked as though something had tried to bury it, as it was covered with dust. He thought, "If some animal killed this rabbit it would be eaten. It wasn't." He headed home convinced that he had evidence of some major migration. This was certainly news. His plan was to get a photographer to come take pictures, talk to the border authorities, then write the story of a lifetime.

The Wall

Chapter 5

In the early morning, after hours of sleepless tossing and turning, the president decided he needed comforting. His mind was spinning like a top. He knew he would not be able to sleep until the morning light, when he would have to rise and face a new day, tired and groggy. It was no good. He climbed out of his nest and went to the end of the branch where there was vine intended to be his fire escape. He used it for many reasons but never, so far, for a fire. He slid down the vine and scampered off into the bushes before he could be seen by his secret service guards. When the coast was clear, he crossed the park, swam the reflecting pool, and came out in one of the older, poorer neighborhoods left from the previous civilizations. Dodging from trash can to tree, to tricycle, he made his way to number 317 Porcupine and crept up onto the porch. He could have thrown a pebble to try to get attention and been invited in, but he did not want any of the snoopy neighbors to check on the strange noise. Instead, he climbed up one of the branches that held the porch roof. The roof was beyond his reach and the gutter made it a few more inches away, way too far to reach. He would have to jump. The problem was there was no place to put his feet to push off. He thought if he wrapped his rear legs around the branch and stretched his body he might just be able to reach the edge of the gutter. Holding his body as stiff as he could, he managed to grab hold with one of his front paws just as his rear legs began to cramp and he had to let go. It left him hanging there by one paw. He knew if he dropped he was sure to be heard and someone would come to investigate. He had made a bad decision. If he had thrown the pebble, he would be on the ground where he could make a quick escape. Now he was hanging with nowhere to go but a long way down. He could feel the gutter loosening and creaking. His swinging was going to tear it away from the roof. In the crotch of the tree above his position a light came on and a shadow appeared. There was a pause. Was someone calling the police? Then something soft and pink was hanging next to him. It was a pillow. With his free paw he clutched it and then grabbed it with the other. From there he was able to pull himself up onto the roof and into the arms of Tamara. "Tommy, thank goodness you are OK. Why didn't you call? I could have let you in."

"I didn't think of that. Next time I'll give it a try," he said feeling very contrite.

She led him into the her nook and into her bed where she petted his mane and caressed his ears while he told her of all the horrible things facing him in the coming days. He had no idea what to do. There was a drought in the West. The East had a drug epidemic. The South was dealing with police issues, and the whole country was worried about terrorists. She listened with the ear of one who is more interested in the teller than the final outcome of the problems. She was wiser than those who pretended to have the answers and knew there were no final solutions, only temporary answers that placated some until the next bombshell. As he ran the list he realized that he was not worried now. Now he was in his lover's arms and things were good. Soon he was sound asleep.

She whispered in his ear just before daybreak, waking him so that he could get back to his home and prepare for the morning's press conference. At first he was confused. Having traveled so much recently, it took him a few moments to remember where he was. He felt relaxed for the first time in quite a while. Tamara's bed was like a safe zone, where he could once again feel Tamarin urges for warmth and comfort and, in mating season, sexual release. She was not in heat so he did not have that distraction and that was probably a good thing. He couldn't afford to be too relaxed. Retracing his steps, except for hanging off the gutter, he was back in his room when the alarm went off at six o'clock. When he went down to breakfast as usual. *The Pandora's Box*, the capitol newspaper was at his place as usual. But what was on the front page was not usual. It was a picture of him hanging from Tamara's gutter and a story about how a prowling tamarin was photographed by a security camera the previous night. There had been complaints of prowlers in the neighborhood so the Neighborhood Watch had set up the device to try to catch the perpetrator. The caption was vague, saying only the police were following leads in the investigation. His heart sank. He knew that the Carnivore Party, which tried to portray him as unprincipled, would be trying to prove this was the president and he could not be trusted. In two hours he would have to face the press and there would be questions. There would certainly be questions. The phone rang and he was quite certain he knew who was calling.

The Rabbit family had been on the trail for two weeks now. They had all lost weight, their ribs were beginning to show and their coats looked moth eaten. They were tired to the bone. Each day they struggled to find food. June, the grandmother, had doubts about being on the right trail. She knew if they had taken a wrong turn somewhere and there were no markings, they would all end up as buzzard bait. Someday they would be just another bunch of bleached bones. Some animal would come by and create a story trying to explain their presence. During the day, as they found shelter from the blistering sun, they hovered in silence, each with his own thoughts of how to cope with the coming days and his possible mortality. It was getting desperate and they all knew it, but to speak about it would only make matters worse for the others.

That evening, as they looked for something to eat farther off the trail, Jeremiah thought he could see a faint glow low on the horizon to the north. At first he thought it might be a lightning storm but as he watched he became convinced that it was artificial light. It had to be civilization. He kept looking, not wanting to create any false hope for the family, but wanting at the same time to share what he thought was good news. During the next few nights it did seem to get brighter, and he wondered if any of the others had seen it. A few mornings later, as the sun turned the black sky to a lovely pink, they came upon an arroyo that had recently held some water. There was still some grass growing in the shade of a mesquite. This put a bit of spring back in their hop. They had a long way to go and there might be stretches with very little food, but they were trail hardened and the green grass gave them reason for hope. They began to see bits of litter, signs that they were on a trail. When the sun was unbearable, they sought shelter in some sage brush that had collected under a pine. Jeremiah asked if anyone had seen anything unusual the previous evening. Everyone said they had but hesitated to say anything, fearing being mistaken and promoting false hope. As she sat looking around at the group June, the grandmother, suddenly broke into uproarious laughter. In a few seconds they were all laughing and rolling on the ground until they were worn out and fell into a lovely silence and slept.

They slept all day except for Rufus, who had been thinking that, although things were looking up, they needed a plan. They still had a long way to go and what would happen when and if they did get to the border? How would they get across? And then what? So far they were driven by the desire for something better than what they were born into. Something that did not make life a daily struggle until the day you were dressed in some finery you never wore during your lifetime and the family said things about you which were never told to your face. But since he had no idea what he would find at the border, it was difficult to be rational. Any plan was certain to not conform to the actual circumstances. Perhaps the most difficult part of the trip would be when it was over.

Julie was never a very good sleeper. As a kitten, she had

dreams that kept her awake and made her cry until one of her parents came to hold her. On this day she was having such a dream, but it was a good one. In it she was at a picnic where she and lots of other young rabbits were playing hide and seek. The dream was so vivid that she began to her move about in her sleep. Suddenly she gave a loud squeal, awakening the whole family. Jenny hopped over to thinking that she must be having a nightmare. Julie was holding her back paw between the front two and crying. "What is it? her mother asked, "What happened?"

"I don't know. I think something stung me."

Jenny took the paw for a better look and saw that it was beginning to swell. Then she saw what stung her daughter. Under a branch, hiding from something much bigger than itself, was a black scorpion with its young riding on its back. June called to the others who came over wondering what was such a big deal about a dream.

June, Julie's grandmother, got to work with Jenny digging a hole, looking for some damp soil. Jeremiah and Rufus found a cactus that had the prickers rubbed off and began to chew into it to find some pulp. The outer layer was tough going but eventually they could taste some damp pulp. Rufus took a mouthful of pulp to where the two does were digging and spit it in. June, using her front paw, stirred the mix into a kind of salve.

Jesse, Julie's brother, who seemed oblivious, hopped off to see what he could find in the open country, making sure to leave a good trail so that he would not get lost on the return. He knew the owls would not be looking for a meal at this time of the day, but he must keep an eye out for hawks. As he hopped from some brush to a hole to a rock, he kept a constant watch on the sky. This was getting a bit monotonous as well as being dangerous. It was more of the same things they had seen along the trail. As he turned to head back to the campsite, he saw a shadow glide by and turned his eyes up to see Hillary Harris Hawk out for her morning sortie. He knew she must have spotted him and would be coming back. He began shaking, knowing she would make short work of a young rabbit like himself. He needed cover fast. Twenty feet away, across an open space that would be perfect for her to grab him, was a rock with an overhang. He made one last look skyward and saw that she had made a turn and was coming back, starting to go into tuck dive. The rock was his only chance. He turned on the speed that jackrabbits are known for and bound across the open space. On the last bounce before the rock he caught his sleeve on a thistle, which spun him around just as Hillary was about to grab him. "Damn," she said to herself. She hit the empty ground where Jesse should have been and bounced back into the air with a quick flap of her lovely brown wings. Jesse tore off the jacket in one quick move and dove for the rock.

He sank there quivering, thinking he should be thankful but not knowing who to thank. He rubbed his legs and felt proud to be a jackrabbit equipped with such marvelous defense equipment. As the shaking subsided, he looked around the space he was occupying. Behind him was something that looked like it could be bone. He scratched at it and soon had it exhumed. Staring back at him were the empty sockets of a rabbit skull, like none he had ever seen. It had a large sagittal crest running down the centerline of the top and two large teeth that protruded forward. He looked into the vacant eyes. Jesse loved stories and this reminded him of one. He asked himself, "What was this thing and how did it get here?" He kept looking into those eyes, waiting for an answer. What was it telling him? Maybe it was that there had been a previous time when his ancestors had held sway in this land. This rabbit had fought battles here, and searched for food here, and hid from his enemies here. Jesse was not alone, but part of the continuum, a very long one, that was evolving all the time. It was a grand story that would go on forever but was not comprehensible, like the stars above that came and went. He wanted to take this story back to his family and tell them but he knew they would not understand. He did not fully understand, but it was important and he felt changed.

He waited for the time between day and night and then found his way back to the rest of the rabbits.

"Where have you been?" they asked. "We were all worried the hawk we saw might have nabbed you."

"I was simply exploring, looking for something to entertain myself," and let it go at that.

Chapter 6

Molly Mallard sat at her console looking for news stories. Nothing jumped out at her. Then she remembered the rumor that Toby had mentioned and wondered if any of the foreign press was covering it. She did a search. In the back pages of the obscure Central Animalia newspaper *El Veridad* was a story about the drought in the central planes and the impact on some of the inhabitants, especially the jackrabbits. She did a search for "jackrabbit migration," then "jackrabbit lemmings," and finally "jackrabbits on the move." There wasn't much. She did find some research about pet rabbits that were put in stressful situations during wars where they were used for experiments and starved. The study found that they became aggressive and tried to attack their keepers. When let loose, they formed large groups and hopped off, devouring everything in their path. She decided it was time to have a look. Before going on assignment she needed to get Mr. Donkey's approval. He was in his office going over that evening's big stories with Ms. Pigchops. Melba Mockingbird, his secretary, let her in.

"Sorry to interrupt," she said, "but this is important. I think there is a major event happening just south of the border. If we don't get on this, one of the local stations is going to get wind of it and we will look like fools for sitting on our paws."

"OK, let's hear it. I'm all ears," said Wonkey.

Molly giggled to herself but didn't dare let him hear as she appraised the large appendages on the top of his head. "Well," She said, "there are reports in some of the Central Animalia press of an invasion of starving rabbits headed for our border. Apparently there is a severe drought in the area and they are having difficulty finding food. When jackrabbits are hungry, they get aggressive and form large groups. When they get to the border they could cause havoc. As you know the border is very porous and guards are in short supply. If this story is true, they could overwhelm the border and fan out all over our country, spreading..." She ran out of what to say and had no idea what the conclusion might be, but all the scenarios she could think of were not good.

Wonkey sat back in his chair and stared at her while Ms. Pigchops was thinking about her career. If she broke this story she would be interviewed on every talk show in the country. She could go to any network and name her price. She would be up there with Walter Wallaby, who secured his reputation after finally calling out the government for its misrepresentation of the Big War. No one questioned why he had accepted the official version for so long. Now he was heralded as one of the greats. "Let her go," she said. "We could use a story like this. There is nothing going on except the possible scandal with President Tamarin, and the pictures are so bad we can't possibly pin him down. The Carnivore Party would love to see us pursue it but, I tell you, if he can prove it wasn't him we will never live it down. Besides, he will treat us like a pariah.

Wonkey rolled his eyes while chewing his cud. It was supposed to make the underlings watching him think that he was in the act of deep consideration, thoughtfully trying to decide, a manager doing what only the best ones could do. Really what he was thinking was, "What a bunch of snakes I am surrounded by. All they think about is their careers. They don't give a damn about what it costs to run this mess." Still, she had a point. *The News* could use a good story. He had some stock options which he could pick up. If this story went world-wide, he could retire and take a university position to teach as an emeritus professor. He was already picturing himself in a cardigan sweater, with his feet on the desk, smoking an unlit pipe, and listening to the co-eds trying to impress him.

"Well," said Molly. "Can I go?"

"I'll have Melba arrange it."

Molly left, quacking to herself all the way down the hall and into the street. She would call Toby as soon as she got home.

After hearing from his press secretary what he could expect at the press conference, the president went to the trapezoid office to make some notes to prepare himself. He would know nothing about the pictures that were going global on the internet. It was just another smear tactic by the Carnivore Party. They were pulling out all the stops to make him look bad before the next election. There were serious issues that needed to be dealt with, but they were more interested in personal attacks. The trouble was, it seemed to work. He mulled over the idea of having the Central Snoop see if they could find any dirt on Marty Moose, the Carnivore frontrunner. He pushed the thought to the back of his mind for later consideration and concentrated on the questions that he would be asked. This story of the invading rabbits was beginning to gain traction. It was moving toward the front page in some newspapers. Journals had scientific studies, the tabloids had pictures of pets being attacked by carnivorous rabbits, and discussions of Central Animalia inferiority on *Coyote News*. Some of the networks were showing old Bugs Bunny cartoons. Weren't most of them invasive species? It didn't matter. "Last one in, close the door." It could get out of hand if he did not take control. It was just the kind of thing that Moose would love to use in the election. Border security, blah, blah, blah. The whole Southwest was dependent on immigration but the rest of the country thought anyone that wasn't a red-blooded Animalian was going to infect their society. Maybe he should give it up and take Tamara off to a Caribbean island to live in peace. If he lost the next election that is certainly what he would do. Enough of this noise.

As for the rabbits, if it was true, he needed to do something, but what? He certainly didn't want to create xenophobic chaos. On the other hand, it could turn into a nightmare if thousands of starving rabbits started showing up at the fence. Rather than go through channels, which always seemed to leak, he decided to call the head of border security for that region and put her on notice that there could be trouble, and that she should call him directly at the first sign of any unusual activity.

He dressed in a serious blue tie, white shirt, and dark jacket and called for his sidecar and driver. As the motorcade sped down Love Thy Neighbor Avenue, he looked forward to being able to tell the press that he had the appropriate authorities looking into the matter. That should hold them for a day or two. They would want to know exactly what he was doing to secure the frontier, and he would assure them that it was secure. They shouldn't jump to any conclusions.

His press secretary was taking questions when he arrived. He went to the bathroom where he found a small artificial tree with the presidential seal, the official pee spot for presidents since Harry Hippo had held the office. President Tamarin wondered how a hippo could lift his leg far enough to relieve himself on a tree. He tried to picture it. There must have been a lot of embarrassing moments. He approached the podium and welcomed them all. He asked them to keep their questions to serious matters. He did not want to get into personality disputes during the campaign season. He knew the players and who would give him the questions he wanted to answer. He deflected those about his nighttime visitation, said the rabbit story was only a rumor, and the trade deal was just waiting on congressional approval. When he was done he felt that he had accomplished his mission, but it would not last. The photos of him trying to get into Tamara's were too fuzzy to prove anything but the Carnivores were going to get all the press they could out of the bunny business.

The Wall

Chapter 7

Marty Moose climbed off his Exercycle after the odometer told him that he had ridden ten miles in thirty minutes. He was pretty sure that the reading was optimistic and the machine needed calibrating, but he used the figures anyway when discussing his prowess. His reputation was important to him. He saw how the other moose let themselves go and found it disgusting. How could they expect to get a cow interested if they looked more bovine than moose-like. After the peddling, he went out to his pool and swam a few laps to relax, then stretched out on a chaise lounge where he found a cold covfefe waiting for him. He wanted to look his best during the upcoming campaign season when he would be seen debating Tommy Tamarin. Who could tell what kind of shape he was in under all that fur? Marty envied him a bit for the fact that Tommy could get away with overeating and no one would know. Still, he felt very smug knowing that he was a fine specimen of a moose. Later he would go back the gym to have a full body massage and his rack polished.

The news was all good, or should we say bad, for President Tamarin. First there were the pictures of him hanging from a gutter, if you could believe the tabloids. Then there was this business with the rabbits trying to sneak across the borders. That was playing right into Marty's hooves. In fact, he couldn't have scripted it better. He had been complaining about immigrants for years, how they polluted Animalia with their foreign language and strange food and customs, stealing grazing land from legal citizens. It had a great deal of emotional power and was difficult to counter. Now, with the economy in decline, it was getting more traction. When animals looked at him they could see what a real Animalian should look like. He strove to be that example. He was that example. He would be ready to meet his wealthy backers and advisors that evening, and they would be impressed. When they all sat down in front of their juicy, imported steaks, each one of them would know that he or she had chosen the right animal to back as the presidential nominee for the Carnivore Party. What they wouldn't know was that his had been especially prepared so that he could chew it with teeth that were designed to eat plants.

The other big question that no one wanted to discuss, was the population. Already the infrastructure of the country was ready to bust. The roads to the grazing lands and watering holes were jammed. On weekends things came to a standstill. Fights broke out. Tempers were being tested. Litters were litters. They were a certain size and nothing could be done about that. When the urge to copulate struck, as it did every spring, more often for some, the animals all did it. But this Central Animalia thing was different. Those animals seemed to have bigger litters, and more than once a year. If they came to the this land that Marty idealized, how would the roads be then? And what about the schools? Class sizes were already too big. Building schools would take more taxes. Pocketbook issues citizens could understand. If they didn't understand the fact that they were slowly being overwhelmed by too many creatures trying to inhabit the same planet, they could understand the money. It was time to bring up the issue. It could get ugly. His enemies would accuse him of being a racist and compare him to every tyrant since Genghis Chan. But if he could convince enough of them that more animals meant more expense, he would be able to win. He needed an event that his supporters could point to as proof his position made him worthy of leading the greatest country, one to win over the unconvinced, and something that the press couldn't ignore. He was quite sure that event was about to deliver itself to his front door.

Simon Salamander went about his business taping the

reports of fires, drug arrests, bomb threats, and political upheavals around the world. They were meticulously filed for later reference. The promising ones were fed to Mr. Donkey for analysis. If he thought they were newsworthy, he put Ms. Pigchops into the loop so that she could do follow-up. This day a story came in from a stringer they sometimes used in Uzbekistan, who had been sent by *Euroblab*, the European news network, to cover the annual osprey fishing tournament in Baja. While there, he had run into another reporter named Garland. Garland had told him about something his wife had seen, which he was not able to explain but might be of interest. "Probably nothing," he said, but hundreds of rabbits, maybe thousands, may be traveling north towards the border. Might be a big story. Sure, there were always rabbits in the desert, but so many, and all headed in the same direction?"

Garland told him it was probably caused by the drought and food shortage.

"Yeah, but if thousands of rabbits show up at the border without visas, what will happen? There are vigilantes who may take advantage of the situation. And there are plenty of hungry coyotes that would love to fill up on fresh bunny."

The stringer sent what little he knew to Simon who thought it did not bear recording and left it in the ethernet. Simon was a slow thinker but a story with no corroboration was no story at all. It would be a waste of time to save it.

One of the stringers, Henry Hedgehog, on the other hand, could see that if there was some truth to the story and thousands of rabbits were headed to the border, he might get the scoop. He took a bus to Ca Pat and the ferry across the gulf to Topolobumpo. From there, he caught the train to Enchilada. Going through Hummingbird Canyon, he had time to reflect on what the rabbits must be feeling and the stress they would be under. Being from a poor country, he understood how hard life could be. He himself had grown up in poverty. His family often did not have enough to eat and had to resort to dead bugs and rotten fruit. He watched as his brothers and sisters turned into skin and bone. A skinny hedgehog is not a pretty sight.

By the time he got off the train and found a bus heading toward Animalia Central Ciudad, he was convinced that this was going to be the story of his career. It was a disaster in the making. If enough pressure was brought on the animal kingdom, surely these poor critters could be helped. Garland had told him about where they had been seen but he would need to do some reconnaissance to find their present location, but first he would need transportation. If he waited 'til they arrived at the border the whole press corps would be there with the eyes of the world, waiting.

Molly took a red-eye out of Ronny Reptile Airport and arrived in Central Animalia City the next morning. From the Jose Jaguar Airport she went to the hotel that Melba had booked for her, wondering where this would all lead. Animal rights were something she felt strongly about, but she worried about their headline grabbing ability. It was strange that every animal at one time or another would be put in the position of having their rights abused by some authority but until it was personal, they could not identify others in that situation. If this was a case of starving rabbits trying to save themselves and their families, shouldn't governments be on their side instead of using them as a political football? It seemed most of these jokers in office only knew how to use a situation to further their own agenda. Those in need were just chess pieces on a board. She hoped she could put the animal face on this story.

Using her new language skills, she searched for a guide that was willing to help her look for the rabbits. She started by looking on the Internet for nature guides but all she found were birding guides. She wasn't looking for birds, and being a bird herself, that seemed a bit redundant. She began to quack to herself which helped her think. "Of course," she thought, "what I need is a hunting guide. But can I do it? Can a duck hire a hunting guide?" She thought about the cartoons she watched as a chick, Elmer Fudd trying to shoot Donald Duck. Maybe there were rabbit hunting guides. It was a terrible idea and all hunting had been eliminated in Animalia back in the human days, but it was still part of the culture here, even though many opposition to it as being barbaric. She did another search. There it was: "Bugle Beagle for hire, best nose in the business." There was an address not too far from her hotel. Molly went downstairs and asked the desk clerk where she would find it. She landed on the roof of an old, seedy building. It looked as if business probably wasn't too good from the looks of things. If this building was in Animalia it would have been condemned long ago. Most of his clients probably never came to the office. They would meet in the field. Maybe she should have called. Now she was here. No time for second thoughts. She wasn't going to leave.

The frosted glass window said, "Anteater Exterminations, #539." Did she have the right building? There was one way to find out. She tapped on the glass with her beak. No answer. She tried again and listened. She thought she could hear snoring. She quacked as loud as she could. There was movement inside and then footsteps. Then the door opened and a black nose appeared.

"Woof, yes, can I help you?"

"Is this the office of Bungie the beagle?

"There's no Bungie. Just me, Bugle. Can I help you?"

"Are you an exterminator or a hunting guide?"

"Depends on what you are trying to exterminate. If its insects, I'm afraid that group went out of business. If it's bunnies, you've come to the right place."

"Neither," she said. "May I come in?"

"Sorry," he said.

The office was tiny, barely big enough for the two of them. He pushed his dirty food and water bowls aside to make room for her to squat. Then he sat on an old furry rag that must have been slept on for years without ever seeing a washing machine. It gave the room a strong doggy odor which he tried to relieve by having the window open a crack.

"Sorry for the mess. I don't get to many clients coming here. Never had a duck. Usually they're other dogs that have a lousy sense of smell and couldn't track an elephant if it was in the next room."

He was old and well fed and looked like he rarely chased anything except his food bowl. Maybe this was a mistake. She explained to him why she had come to Central Animalia and why she had sought him out.

"Would you be interested?" she asked.

He asked her what area they would be searching for these rabbits.

She asked him about his fee.

"I get fifty pesos a day plus expenses, food and transportation."

She worried about the food part. This boy looked like he could run up a hefty tab. He got her phone number, a retainer, and told her to give him a day or so and he would arrange things. After she left, he picked up the phone. It might be dangerous hiring a hawk to look for rabbits, but he needed to find them quickly before they got to the border and Molly lost her chance for an exclusive.

The Wall

Chapter 8

Millie Millipede, head of border security, was a holdover from the previous administration. She had worked her way up through the ranks by stepping over other, more deserving post seekers, using the influence and money that backers were willing to supply given her tough stand on border security. Since then she had won the confidence of her bosses by doing a good job. When she took over, corruption was rampant. Food crumbs were left to distract guards who were not paid much and despised as thugs by those they caught trying to enter the country illegally. She had fought for decent pay and made sure the guards were trained in the art of dealing with desperate people. The tide on this issued ebbed and flowed, depending on who was in charge at the top, and right now there wasn't much of a push. It didn't suit her to be an overseer of an organization that was on hold. She liked being in the news and hoped for the changes that would give her that opportunity. Each morning, while polishing her star, she wondered when she would have the chance to stand in front of a camera and show her country what a stellar officer they had keeping them safe. When the call she had been waiting for came, it did not come from whom she expected. For that reason she was put in a position of having to make a very difficult decision, one that would haunt her dreams for years to come.

Marty needed an issue his backers could support enthusiastically enough to donate to his campaign, lots of money, and something that the dim-witted public could understand. If he could just get proof of invading bunnies, he would have his issue and could ride it right into office. If he could show he was taking steps ahead of the president to deal with an issue, it would make him look presidential, something he had been accused of not being. He wanted to drop this on the assembly tonight to get his backers excited. After toweling off, he went to his office and looked up a contact who could help in this effort. There she was, Millie Millipede. He had pulled strings to get her into her present position just for such an opportunity. Having the right people beholden to you was the key and something that President Tamarin did not seem to understand. He had her private number so there would be no record of the call.

When Millie saw who the call was from on the ID she considered not answering. She had met Marty and found him to be egotistical and difficult. In her mind's eye she could see him chewing away, swamp weed hanging out of his maw, while thinking he was the most beautiful thing on earth. She wondered how anything so big and dumb could get so far in life. Size, she thought. It's just size. Perhaps that was why she had never gone further than this, chief border guard. She knew if she didn't answer he would find a way to contact her using a congressman or senator that she could not ignore. She hit the button and put the phone to her ear.

"Millie, how are you? I heard you were having knee replacement. Did they get the right one?"

"Asshole," she thought but said nothing.

"Say, I am sure you are aware of this story of the Central Animalian rabbits' invasion of our border. I was wondering if you had seen anything to corroborate this story."

"No, haven't seen anything yet. I have heard some rumors. How could you not? But, so far, there is no sign of any rabbits other than the usual traffic."

Marty liked the word "invasion" and decided to use it from

here on when discussing rabbits and the border. "Have you sought any intel on this?"

"No, there has been none."

"What the hell are you waiting for? I'd have your officers over the border, searching every nook and hole to find them. Are you going to wait until they are burrowing under your fence, invading your back yard?"

Millie took a deep breath, "Sir, we have no reason to believe..."

Marty cut her off, "If you refuse to get on this, I'll get you the proof you want," and hung up.

Millie started to consider what Marty had said, and then the options. She would need all of her legs to count the ways. In the end she decided to make the most difficult choice. She did nothing.

For Marty, waiting was not an option. He needed something to show his supporters. He found the name of the Central Animalian newspaper that had originally broken the story, *La Verdad*. There must be someone there who spoke English. He dialed the number.

"Bueno."

"Hablas Inglés?"

"Yes, what can I do for you?"

Marty told the operator to whom he wished to speak.

She told him the reporter was Garland Gila and he was out of the office, but she would have him call back, then asked for Marty's name and phone number.

"Look, this is important. He needs to call me back right away."

"Yes sir. Who shall I say called?"

"Just have him call this number as soon as he gets in."

Marty hated waiting.

He thought, *the hell with waiting. I can't wait. If the rabbits get to the border before I have time to get my plan in place I will have wasted a golden opportunity. President Tamarin will probably grant them all asylum before the congress has time to act. Once they are in we'll never find them. They will spread all over the country and the media will move onto the next story, which will bore all the readers into hibernation.*

If he could get some of his supporters to be guarding the border when the rabbits arrived they could make a stand. They would require coaching. It needed to look like the rabbits were the aggressors and Animalians were just defending the homeland. He knew just the one to get the ball rolling, Ronnie Roadrunner.

Ronnie's office was on the other side of town but, being a roadrunner, he was able to quickly get through the traffic to Marty's office. Marty sat behind a large, but empty, mahogany desk in his architect designed swamp. Ronnie wondered how the moose could keep his work-space so neat. His own was covered with scraps of paper and lists. Sticky notes covered his computer so that the screen was no longer visible. He made sure that from the backside these could not be seen so that it looked like he used it. In fact it was not even plugged in.

Behind Marty on the wall was a stuffed moose head. Hunting animals had been outlawed in Animalia since humans roamed the earth, but Marty thought it would intimidate anyone seeing it. In fact, he told anybody he wanted to impress that it was a relative and he kept it just as some animals might keep photos of ancestors.

His boss sat him down. "Ronnie, I want you to locate as many angry animals as you can and put them up in a convention center near the border. I will make all the arrangements. Once that's done, I will fly down and conduct some training sessions. This cannot look like rabid animals let loose on defenseless rabbits. Think of it as saving the country from unimaginable perils and we are the heroes."

"Where do I find these angry animals?"

"I think if you call the local Carnivore Party leaders in the border towns, they will be able to give you lists of names of those animals that are violently anti-immigrant. Come up with a list of questions to screen out the whackos and put together a list of a couple hundred volunteers. Of course, we don't know how many rabbits we are going to be dealing with but that should be enough to show them we are serious.

"I'll get hopping right away." And he was out the door.

Chapter 9

Hillary Harris Hawk was chewing the head off a rattlesnake when she got the call.

"Hi Hillary, it's Bugle. How's business?"

" I'm up to my beak in blood and guts. How are you?"

Bugle commented that there seemed to be a bad connection, but he had a job for her if she could squeeze it in. He told her where and what she should be looking for and asked her to please not eat any of them. She thought, "What's one rabbit more or less?" But she agreed to let them be if she found them. Having eaten the best part of the snake, she dropped it and took off in the direction she hoped to find the quarry. A strong north wind made flying close to the ground difficult. Higher up things were better and she surmised if there were hundreds of these rabbits they should not be hard to spot.

As she flew toward the border she thought about the best flight pattern to find bunnies trying sneak into Animalia. They would travel at night which would make spotting them difficult. During the day they would seek shade. She couldn't be sure where they would try to cross but they would probably look for a remote area. This could take weeks. She would need a lot of luck.

On the third day of her search she saw a single rabbit hopping about. She made a dive on it hoping to be able to hold it for interrogation. Just as she was about to grab it the bunny was pulled out of its path by something and she missed it. When she came closer for a better look, it dashed under a rock. She hovered overhead for some time but it must have seen her because it did not emerge. She wondered if it might be a young one that had left the group to go explore. She made ever larger circles to find others. Yes, there were more, but not many. It looked to be one family. She spent an hour looking to see if there were more families nearby, then flew off after deciding this was all just one family of lost bunnies.

Bugle was having his afternoon nap when Hillary called to tell him that she was not finding anything unusual and did he want her to continue looking. Bugle was beginning to think maybe his client was barking up an empty tree but it was too early to give up.

When Ronnie arrived at the El Pesto, he rented an office and immediately began to calling local Carnivore Party leaders to put together a list of contacts. Once that was done, he rented a factory building that had once made trucks. The company had moved to the other side of the border leaving the building empty and falling to ruin. He put ads in the local free papers, put up posters, and started making calls. He offered a small daily stipend and free coffee and donuts for the training session that was to take place on the weekend. When he arrived at the factory an hour before the appointed time, there was already a line of rats, vultures, and sidewinder rattlesnakes down the street. This was beyond Ronnie's greatest expectations. He couldn't wait to tell Marty. He let them wait in the cold while he went inside to arrange the food on tables and put up training posters. When the doors opened, the rats smelled the food and attacked the tables, upsetting the boxes of neatly stacked donuts. Fights broke out over the jelly filled and jimmies covered. Some of the less aggressive rodents, happy to take the plain, old-fashioned ones, slinked off to corners where they could eat away from the mayhem.

After the food was gone, some of the rats left and others

began to look for mating possibilities with much butt sniffing. Ronnie let out a squawk that got their attention. When a scratchy version of the national anthem began over the loud - speaker, the crowd came to attention and began to sing. They said the pledge of allegiance, which was hardly ever used these days, but they all knew it from their youths. He ordered them to sit and listen while the ushers handed out armbands identifying them as official border patrol supernumeraries. Then he went over the day's training activities and handed out the walkie-talkies they were to use to communicate with each other. There was more commotion over this, a free radio. Then he informed them they would have to return them after their assignment was completed. This caused some grumbling but most of them soon came to terms with the temporary condition of their assignment. Meanwhile, Henry Hedgehog found his way in and took a seat. He was also surprised to see the turnout. He had begun to think this was going to be a dead end, not worth covering, which clearly was not the case. He wondered how President Tamarin would respond. His role as commander-in-chief was being usurped by Marty, but what could he do to prevent it without angering a large number of his constituents?

Marty Moose came onto the stage to much cheering and applause. He held his hoofs up for quiet after basking in the glow for several minutes. "Thank you all for coming today. It is great to see so many patriotic citizens standing up for their country and saving the purity of what it means to be an Animalian. This is an invasion. We are under siege from infected foreigners which wish to destroy our way of life. The government refuses to deal with this situation so we must. Your children and every generation that comes after you will remember what you are about to do, and thank you. You will go down in history as the patriots, every bit as great as the founders of our blessed land. Once this scourge has been driven back, I will lead us to a brighter future and restore the greatness that we all expect. Prepare to be heroes. My friend Ronnie will give you your assignments and tell you what to expect once the enemy is at the fence."

He thanked them again and left to visit one of his wealthy supporters where he would watch the news coverage of the coming event. Henry fought his way through the crowd to get to the stage before Marty could get away. There were many angry comments as he pushed others in his haste, but he kept going. When he did get to the back of the stage, it was only to see Marty slipping into a limousine and being whisked away. He jotted down the license number, hoping to find out where he was going. Maybe he still could get an interview.

The Wall

Chapter 10

Tamara finished her shift at the hospital, having completed her rounds. She felt exhausted. The day had begun twelve hours earlier with scrubbing up for cardinal surgery. A mother cardinal delivered one of her chicks to the emergency room after one of the other chicks had kicked it out of the nest. It was now resting. As tired as she was, she needed a walk to clear her head and relax before she called Tommy. She hoped he would have time to see her, but he was also under stress with Marty Moose playing up this rabbit thing.

She headed for the park, away from the street lights and noise, following an ancient path worn by deer. Then she climbed a tree and hopped from limb to limb. It felt good to use the abilities that came to her as a birthright. As the day's work slipped out of her consciousness, she relaxed and was ready to make the call. She had his direct line so she did not get filtered out by some bureaucrat. Tommy picked up on the second ring. She knew he must be alone. Yes, he did want to see her. The day had been nothing but bad news. He needed to get away also. He would get there as soon as he could. She took her time getting back to her nest, leaving the door unlocked.

Tommy finished the day in a meeting with his press secretary who was telling him he was ceding this issue of the rabbits to Marty by not making more of an effort to deal with it. The president responded that he was dealing with a water shortage problem and this was just a distraction. "We have no idea how many there are, where they are, or even if there is an invasion." The secretary replied that it did not matter whether or not it was real, it was an opportunity to look presidential and

63

get his face in the media, to be the commander.

His constituents wanted a leader, and right now, Marty was looking more like that leader. Tommy agreed that something had to be done, but what? The secretary told him he had to move soon. Marty had his people in place and this whole thing could come to a head any day. The president was left with the dilemma and no clear solution. If he overreacted, he could have a humanitarian nightmare on his hands. If he did nothing and there was a rabbit invasion, Marty would surely be the next president.

This time he used the door. Tamara was resting on her nest. He curled up next to her and began to tell her about his problem. "If I send the military in, it will look like a war. If I do nothing, I will look weak."

Tamara told him that he needed to get his mind off it for a while and a solution would become evident. He couldn't see how that would happen, but he did need a break.

"Want to see my tattoo?" she asked.

"I didn't know you were getting one."

She rolled over on her back and parted the fur under her third nipple. It was ten different animals which would not ordinarily be seen together, in a circle, holding paws, hands, hooves, or whatever, as if in a dance. In the center of the circle was a mule playing a lute. Tommy looked at the scene and knew why he loved Tamara. "It's beautiful," he said, "really beautiful."

The next morning they both looked like they he'd been in a barroom brawl. Their beautiful coats were matted and full of twigs loosened from the nest during the night. They licked each other until they each looked presentable and went their separate ways feeling ready to face the day.

Tamara thought about Tommy's situation. She worried about him. He was losing focus on what he wanted to accomplish during his administration. His whole presidency could crash and he would be remembered as a failure. She cared for him too much to allow that to happen. She went to work wondering what she could do to help. By lunchtime she had made a decision, went home, packed her bag with medical and hiking supplies, and called Vulture Airlines.

Molly had heard nothing from Bugle in days. Spending time in the Central Animalia City was fine. She did a bit of shopping for relatives, saw some historic sights, went to the natural history museum where she gazed at ancient human mummies. But in the back of her mind was the thought that there was a story that wasn't getting written. It was passing her by and she would forever regret it if the events occurred and she missed them. She left her Rent-a-Nest determined to get some hard answers.

The office door was closed with no sign of Bugle. She thought *this dog could use some lessons in public relations. How was anyone to know he was in business?* She pecked at the door. Nothing. She pecked a few more times and thought she heard some stirring. The door opened and he stood staring at her as if she were a stranger.

"May I come in?" she asked. She had obviously woken him.

"So what have your eyes in the sky found?"

Bugle told her about the single rabbit that Harriet had seen and that she hadn't given up. It was a great deal of territory to cover. Molly reminded him she was looking for a mass migration, and if all the rabbit were there as the reports said they were, they should not be too difficult to spot.

Bugle reiterated that it was a vast area. She said maybe they should go and see if they could find anything. He said that was probably not a good idea.

"Don't you trust that nose of yours which is famous as one

of the best"?

It had been a long time since Bugle had done any of his own searches. He wondered if he could stand up to the rigors. Was he getting too old? Would he make a fool of himself? His reputation was made on work done years ago and survived on the old stories. The young gumshoes were making their own reputations and his was being eclipsed. If he could find these rabbits, he could coast on the publicity for a few more years. When Molly pulled a beef bone that she bought on the black market out of her purse and showed it to him, he said, "OK."

"We'll have to rent an ATV and take supplies necessary to survive on the desert for a few days. I'll take care of that. You be here at eight tomorrow." She left the office convinced they were finally making progress and she would get her story.

The desert of Northern Central Animalia gets very little rain. When the rain does come, it falls in torrents, filling the normally dry riverbeds to the point of overflowing in a few minutes. The rabbits had chosen an unfortunate spot to rest on one of the last nights of their sojourn. They picked it because it provided some morsels of vegetation, which were hard to come by in this rugged country. They heard the storm coming but it sounded so far away they never thought it would reach them, and rain was such a rarity, they almost couldn't remember what it was. When it came, it was in such measure that they were in inches of water immediately. Then they were floating, whisked away in the stream. Jeremiah's first reaction was to grab Julie and scramble up the bank to look for higher ground. As he turned back to see where the others were, he ran into Rufus, then Jenny, and finally June. The sky had turned into a black waterfall so his sight was useless. It was only through touch that his family could be identified. As each member was accounted for he felt relief. After June he went to the river edge to look for Jesse. In the noise and confusion it would be easy to miss him. He went back up the bank and found the rest of the family huddling under a sage bush. During a flash of lightning, he saw the fear in their wide eyes. He was afraid to ask but he had to. "Where is Jesse?" There was no response. "Did anyone see what happened to him?" He knew the answer even as he asked the question. He knew it would be useless to wander off looking for him until he could see. Right now they needed to stick together. Jenny was comforting Julie. He felt the loneliness of the lost and the guilt of the responsible.

By morning, the rain had stopped and the sun came back to return life on the desert to normal. Jenny said they needed to talk, all of them. She had been thinking all night and had come to the conclusion that their only hope to save themselves was for Jeremiah to go for help. The rest would stay put and try to find Jesse. June argued that they needed to stick together. "Suppose Jeremiah has trouble at the border," she said. "We will not know, and will be here waiting until we all perish. Not knowing is the worst part of our condition." It was agreed that they would not split up. Jeremiah said he was going to see if he could find Jesse downriver. Rufus said he would go along and, without waiting for an answer, hopped off following the now subsiding stream.

Chapter 11

Donkey sat at his desk tapping his hoof in agitation, wondering what was happening with his star reporter. It had been a week and she had not filed a single report. He wondered if he had made a mistake sending a duck. They can be so flighty, he thought to himself. She was   where she could not be reached and he was here with no control or oversight. It was intolerable. The more he thought about it, the clearer the answer became. He punched the bottom button on the intercom that connected him to Simon's office. Simon was taping a story and did not want to be interrupted. As he was waiting for Simon to respond he heard a tapping at his widow. It was a pigeon. He waved a hoof to shoe it away but it didn't leave. It kept tapping and he kept shoeing. *Why doesn't it go to a homeless shelter*, he thought. *It probably wants a hand out.*

He opened the window to tell it to get lost but before he could say anything it hopped in and perched on his desk.

"Molly sent me. There is no cell service where she is so she sent me."

"What is going on down there?" He asked.

"She and the P. I. she hired have rented an ATV and are headed to the desert. The harrier they hired had only found one rabbit family so they are going to look for themselves. She says she is sure they will find them before they get to the border, so you should be prepared." With that, he took one of the candies out of the bowlful that Donkey kept on his desk and left.

Donkey hit the bottom button again and yelled into the intercom, "Simon, drop whatever you are doing and get the mobile unit ready to hit the road." Then he hit the second button. "Melba, book a room in El Pesto for me and Simon. We'll need it for a few days" Next, he called Peggy's cell and left a message. She should be prepared to fly to El Pesto for a week. She could find background material on the history of the border and immigration policy, etc. He and Simon would be there in a few days to set up a feed for live coverage.

Molly turned to Bugle, "Do you know how to drive this thing?"

"You better hope so," he replied as they sped through the city, ignoring traffic lights and swerving around pedestrians crossing the street. "There," he barked as he slid the ATV into an illegal parking spot and hopped onto the pavement.

"What are you doing?" Molly shouted.

"I'm getting supplies. We could be on the desert for a week. I've made a list. Want to hear what I've got?"

"Couldn't you have done this yesterday?"

"I wanted to check with you. There is something on the list for every taste: six jelly, eight with jimmies, ten glazed, two plain, a dozen chocolate, and seven latte.

"Wait a minute. You are buying all our food at a donut shop?"

"You don't like donuts? Who doesn't like donuts?"

"I don't eat donuts. I only eat health food. And besides, why did you get an uneven number of lattes? Who would get the extra one? There are two of us. They should all be even numbers."

"We could break it in half," Bugle answered.

"OK, OK," she said. "I'll wait here."

A few minutes later they were back on the road. "Did you

70

get some water?" she asked over the noise of the wind.

"Who needs water?"

"I do. I'm a duck."

Bugle didn't answer but it was not because he wasn't thinking he had made the omission in his list. He hoped his olfactory senses would be up to the job of finding water. It hadn't been tested in a long while. "God," he thought, "I have to get out of the office more often."

He drove through the night woofing down a chocolate donut from time to time to stay alert. Molly tucked her bill under one of her wings, trying to get some sleep, but bouncing over the rutted road made it almost impossible. By morning they had reached the area where Harriet had spotted the rabbit. It was time for Bugle to earn his keep and restore his reputation. He pulled the ATV into a shady area and killed the motor. "This is it," he said. "We are on paw or flipper from here on." He put the supplies in a backpack and his nose to the ground. She told him to wait, she couldn't keep up with a running dog, but it was too late. He was on the trail and didn't even know she was talking.

Molly cursed a bit and then decided that her best bet to keep up was to get into to the air every half hour or so and locate Bugle. Then she could rest and wait for him to progress. Within a few hours he had found the trail and his baying was getting louder. Molly felt relief. Maybe this wasn't going to be a wild goose chase.

Her plan of flying and then searching out Bugle worked until the second day. She found a puddle from a recent rain to paddle around and was having a good time, until she realized she had been there too long. She lifted into the air and began to make circles but there was no Bugle to be seen. "I must have missed him," she thought. She found the puddle again and started to make ever-expanding circles, quacking, hoping to get his attention. She stopped flapping and glided to cut down the noise. Far off she thought she heard a dog. She descended, flying close to the ground in that direction. When she saw him, he seemed to be hurt. He was curled up in a ball, licking one of his back feet. Terrible thoughts went through her mind. What can I do to help a wounded dog?

She landed next to him and asked what had happened. He told her he had the trail; he was sure of it. But he hadn't been paying attention to where he was walking and stepped on a thorn which was now embedded in his paw. Unfortunately, dog's teeth are not very good at grabbing small things like thorns so he had no way of removing it. Molly took a look and could see it stuck between two of his toes.

"Let me see what I can do," she said. She worked her beak in between the pads until she felt it with the nail on the tip of her beak, and grabbed onto it. She pulled so hard that when it slipped out of her grasp, she tumbled over backwards and landed in a heap. "Let me try again," she said, dusting herself off. This time she pushed her beak in as far as she could, until Bugle squealed. Biting down as hard as she could, she twisted and pulled. Again, she tumbled over backwards, but this time there was a cactus thorn in her beak. Bugle was immediately on all fours, hopping around and yipping with joy. He put a paw on Molly's back and licked her beak and head. "Don't get all sloppy on me," she said, but inside she was smiling and glad to be here with this old hound.

Jeremiah and Rufus spent the day trying to find Jesse. They hopped along the river-bank hoping to find him along the shore. The river had fallen almost as fast as it had risen so they were quite sure he would have been able to pull himself out. There were plenty of snags he could have grabbed to keep from being washed away, but there was no sign of him, not even a bit of fur. Rufus said that could be good or bad. It might mean he had drowned, or it might mean he had gotten out of the river and was wandering. All the time they called his name as loud as rabbits can, to no avail. As the sun began to set, they realized they were a long way from where the others were camped and decided to rest for a while before beginning the trip back. They found a spot that had soft river sand and made themselves comfortable. Rufus pulled out his pipe, "June hates this thing so this is the perfect opportunity." They sat quietly, each lost in his own thoughts. Then Jeremiah said he had no regrets. They had done what they had to do. Life in Central Animalia had become unbearable. Someday maybe they could return. One never knew what was around the next corner. Then he said he hoped Jesse hadn't suffered too much if he had died in the river. The night came in like a shroud and the stars filled the sky. All was blackness around them except the occasional glow from the corncob pipe Rufus was puffing on.

"What was that?" Said Rufus.

They both listened. Nothing. "There it is again."

Jeremiah said he heard something also. There was silence. Then there was a loud quacking and a duck calling, "Are there any rabbits about?"

They both began to thump their back legs and holler, "Over here!"

Soon they could tell it was an engine they heard and it was getting closer. They kept thumping and hollering. They could see a light coming their way. They hopped up and down to be more visible.

When the ATV pulled up and they saw it was occupied by a beagle, they started to run, but Molly called to them, "It's OK. We have been looking for you and are here to help."

Jeremiah and Rufus stopped at a distance and looked back. "Please," said Molly, "We are reporters and have been trying to find you to get your story. Where are all the others?"

73

Jeremiah explained how they had left the family to look for Jesse. The rest were not far away waiting for them to return, hopefully with the lost rabbit.

"No, I mean all the other rabbits that are headed for the border."

"What others? We haven't seen any others."

Molly looked at Bugle. Bugle looked at Molly. Then they both began to laugh with a few quacks and howls mixed in. When they had settled down to the realization that there was no invasion about to happen, they offered to give the bunnies a ride back to the rest of the family but were told it wasn't far. They could hop. Rufus asked Bugle how he had found them. Molly answered that before it was dark they had seen the smoke, must have been the pipe, and thought it must be an animal sending signals. They had taken a compass course and headed in that direction. Bugle told them that they were very close to El Pesto and would be there the next day. Molly wished them good luck and said she hoped they would find Jesse. She said she needed to get to where there was phone service to let her boss know there was no story. Bugle started the engine, they said their goodbyes, and headed back to Central Animalia City. Rufus and Jeremiah decided to give up the search and get back to the rest of the family with their tale and the bad news about Jesse.

As she and Bugle bounced over the trail back towards civilization, Molly considered all that had happened. There were the rabbits who lived in a state of abandonment with no country caring about their welfare. There was the news about how this whole story had exploded out of control. And now that it had, how were she and Mr. Donkey going to squash it. If they admitted that it was just one family of rabbits trying to find a better life, it would look like they were trying to make a big story out of a minor event. They could try for an animal interest story but Wonkey would never go for it. Then there were the politics and Marty Moose. How was he going to play this? She thought maybe if she got hold of Mr. Donkey right away, he could put the brakes on the whole thing and let it die. Let Marty and President Tamarin deal with it. Maybe that was the story. When they were near the small village of Cucaracha, she tried her phone. She had a few bars so she dialed Wonkey's cell.

"Hello," he said in his baritone voice. "Molly, is that you?"

She answered that it was and started to explain to him that she had seen the rabbits, but there was only one family.

"Molly, is that you? You've seen the rabbits? How many are there? Molly, you are breaking up."

Molly yelled into the phone but it was no use. He could not hear her.

"Simon, Peggy, and I are on our way," was the last thing she heard.

Chapter 12

Ronnie gathered his troops. Overhead the blistering ball in the sky began to cook the air and everything in it. Moisture formed in his wing pits. It wasn't only the heat. He was beginning to have doubts about this whole operation. They were a motley looking group. He arranged them in rows for inspection. He made sure each one had his Animalia flag patch prominently displayed. When he called for attention, some of them thought it was a signal that more food had been put out and broke ranks. When he had them back in their rows, he told them they must conduct themselves in an orderly fashion. He wasn't sure they had any idea what he meant. They were not to be seen clubbing any of the invading rabbits. They needed to be aware of the cameras at all times. When there was a camera, they should simply talk to the rabbits telling them they needed to go back and were not welcome. They were to space themselves along the fence so that any bunnies trying to dig under it would be near enough to be caught and repelled. Looking at the rows of vacant faces sent a shudder down his spine. Ronnie thought if he had more time he might actually be able to turn them into a disciplined force. But there was no time. The rabbits were getting close and they needed to be there, ready. He told them to go to their posts and released them. There was one problem. He had forgotten to give them assignments. When they got to the fence they realized they had no idea where Ronnie wanted them.

He rode along the fence in the jeep Marty had provided for him, with two large Animalian flags flapping from poles, trying to get his volunteers into position. Peggy and Simon were preparing for the live coverage. Simon had hired a local lighting crew to setting up hundreds of high intensity LEDs to light up the border, which now began to look like a movie set. Since there was no government presence, Peggy was at a loss for someone to interview. She sent one of the cameramen to request one with Ronnie. She was doing a sound check when he arrived. She had one of the make-up moles get him ready while she did herself. With the international fence in the background, they stood together and faced the cameras. Peggy gave some background, telling the audience that in a short time there would be thousands of rabbits trying to enter the country illegally and local citizens had taken the matter into their own paws to try to prevent this from happening. The leader of this group was here with her to explain exactly what they intended to do. She introduced Ronnie, who shifted nervously, not sure what he should say.

"Mr. Roadkill, can you tell us when you expect the arrival of the foreigners?"

"They are not just foreigners. They are invaders."

"Yes, but how soon will they be here at the border?"

"I have no idea," Said Ronnie.

"You are prepared to stay until they arrive no matter how long it takes?"

"We will stay."

"There are rumors that candidate Moose is behind your group and is funding it. Can you tell us if that is true?"

"You'll have to ask him. I have no comment."

"Why can't you tell us if Mr. Moose is supporting this effort?"

Ronnie felt as if he had fallen into the sea and was sinking. He could feel the water as it pressed him closer to the bottom.

The Wall

Tamara worried that she might be too late to help when her flight was rerouted through Otterville on the way to El Pesto. She rented a scooter at the airport and headed to the border. What she saw assured her that she was not too late. Along the fence angry looking rats were baring their teeth and twitching their tail. More networks had sent crews which were looking for good locations to set up their cameras. She stopped a hedgehog to ask him what was the latest estimate of the arrival time. He said there were reports of the rabbits being close but no one had actually seen them so it would certainly be a few hours. He asked her who she was and she told him that she was a doctor who thought she might be of help. There would certainly be casualties when they started trying to enter the country. He told her he was a reporter trying to get an interview with Marty Moose, but had lost him when he left the organizational meeting. He asked her if she was hungry. She realized that she hadn't eaten since leaving the capitol and was starved. They found a diner.

"What are you going to do while you wait?" Henry asked.

"I am not going to wait," she said. "I am going to try to find them and warn them what they will find when they get here."

Henry was incredulous, "You are going into the desert to speak to thousands of desperate rabbits?"

"If it will avoid a disaster, why not?"

Henry realized that this might be the story he was meant to write. "Can I come along?" he asked.

Tamara thought it might be a good idea to have another along and agreed. An hour later they were at the border showing their IDs to the Central Animalia authorities. "Are you sure you want to be going into the desert tonight?" the guard asked. Henry was bigger than Tamara and made the seating a bit tight but he seemed to be someone she could count on if the need arose. They sped down the road, expecting any moment to run into thousands of starving rabbits. Already they had gone as far as a hopping bunny could travel in a day. They couldn't have missed them. Tamara pulled the scooter to the side of the road and killed the engine. "I need a break," she said.

"What do you think? Where are they?" finally able to talk without the noise of the engine. She had no idea. There was nothing but a black sky, empty road, and silence. Then the silence became a growl. It was getting louder. It wasn't an animal. It was a vehicle. They could see the beam from the headlight coming their way. They decided they should hide the scooter and stay out of sight until they could determine who this was. It might be criminals. As the vehicle got closer and they could see the occupants, they stepped into the road to stop it. Sitting in the front seat of the ATV were a duck and a small dog. In the back seat was a young rabbit.

President Tamarin sat back in the Octagon Room, thinking about the day's schedule. His popularity ratings were in the trash barrel and he could see no upcoming event that was going to improve them. In the meantime, he had a bunch of meetings with heads of state, graduation speeches, fund raising dinners, and advisory meetings with his staff. And there was this illegal bunny situation. It could blow up in his face making him look completely incompetent or it might just turn out to be a tempest in a teapot. The intercom buzzed. He pushed button number one, "Yes."

"Phineus is here sir."

Tommy wondered why he had chosen Phineus Fox to be his press secretary. Was it his air of superiority and the fancy education supported by his blue blood lineage? He was proud of making his own way, coming from a humble background and fighting to be on equal footing to those born into the trappings of high society. Still, once in a position of power he had surrounded

80

himself with others who had gotten there through family influence. Phineus was just such a one and he wondered if he really was the best choice. Before he could continue this line of thinking, the secretary sat on the rug in front of Tommy's desk and began to fill him in on what was happening in the press that concerned him. Tommy had already seen all the lead stories on his phone but Phineus had been up since three in the morning combing over the world press releases for anything that might be of interest.

"There was a story in the *South Animalia Sentinel* written by a freelancer by the name of Toby Toad. His name has been associated with the rabbit rumors. In this story he claims he has seen the female companion of President Tamarin, Tamara Tamarin, near the Central Animalia border. He speculates that she may be there as an unofficial representative of the government. Meanwhile, he says that vigilantes are preparing for an onslaught of thousands of starving rabbits trying to enter Animalia illegally.

"Did you send her down there, sir?" Phineus asked.

"I had no idea. It's just like her to take matters into her own paws and run off without consulting me." Tommy said, "I need to see what is happening there for myself."

He immediately pushed number one on the intercom, "Carol, get me Millie Millipede, head of border security in El Pesto, on the line.

Tommy and Phineus stared at each other across the big desk until Carol said Millie was on line two.

"Millie, what the hell is happening there? All I hear is rumors. Now I hear that Marty Moose may be preparing a bloodbath at the border and my friend Tamara may be in the middle of a mess. Would you say the area is secure? Have you seen any evidence of the rabbits?"

Millie assured him all this noise about rabbits was just

"the usual." The "take matters into your own hands" crowd were always ready to do battle. They loved an excuse to show who the real patriots were. "Sir, there has been nothing out of the ordinary that I know of."

That did not allay Tommy's fears. "I want you to cover the El Pesto border today with as many security officers as you can muster on short notice, and set up a control perimeter. Let me know as soon as you have this done. I may come down myself. I think you may have underestimated the seriousness of this situation."

Millie's head began to ache. She was in a difficult situation and Tommy was to blame. She should not be doing anything without orders from her supervisor, but now Tommy, the president, had given her an order. And why did he think he knew more than the officer's whose job it was to oversee the border. At the very least, she needed to let her superiors know what was happening, then she would begin to set up a patrol. But first she needed to get an aspirin.

Bugle saw Tamara and Henry by the side of the path and stopped the ATV. He said to Molly, "This is a strange place to find a Tamarin and a hedgehog."

Tamara was saying something similar to Henry. Tamara asked Molly is she had seen any rabbits besides the one in the back of their ATV. Molly said there was no large group of rabbits. She told Henry and Molly about the lone family and how they had decided to go to El Pesto to inform the authorities and the media that it was a false rumor when they had found Jesse wondering, lost and delirious. They knew he must be the youngster that had gotten separated from the family in the flood and planned to reunite him with his parents at the border. Tamara and Henry asked for directions to the bunny's camp. Bugle and Molly told them they had never actually been to the camp and had only seen Jesse's father and grandfather. The sibling of the young bunny they had with them had been stung by a scorpion and was very sick. They gave the general direction of the camp but could not be specific since the bunnies were on the move. After their information was shared and both parties felt they now knew most of what they needed to know, Bugle and Molly headed off for El Pesto, and Tamara and Henry went to hunt for the family along the border.

It didn't take long. Huge searchlights set up on truck booms crisscrossed the land like so many incandescent turtles. Overhead, helicopters sent beams raining down, while stirring the desert soil into a dust cloud. Ronnie's snakes and rats were everywhere, scrambling about in hopes of being the first to see the invaders. Camera crews from every major news organization were recording their anchors interviewing any animal with a title. Psychologists, sociologists, behaviorists, the mayor of El Pesto, and the governor all got a chance to explain what was about to happen and why. Peggy was finishing what she hoped would be an exclusive with Ronnie. She asked him how he came to take such an interest in refugee rabbits. Ronnie's interest in rabbits went back a long time. In his youth, after the "no carnivore" laws were passed, his mother had taught him to look for dead ones that had been killed on the highway. She told him how it was their civic duty to clean up the roads they ran. All the turkey vultures had to become vegetarians so something had to do it. Still, the thought of hundreds, maybe thousands, of rabbits on the road was a nightmare he couldn't shake. Marty had taken advantage of his psychosis to persuade him that his vision was real. He felt so reverential toward Marty for trusting him that he would never face the truth, namely that he would do anything for Marty Moose.

He repeated the mantra, "I'm here to protect our citizens from foreigners who come and steal our jobs. They bring in diseases and pollute the genetic pool."

Marty watched the interview reclining on a chaise by his friend's pool. When he heard Ronnie mention genetics, he cringed and prayed that his own name would not be mentioned as having anything to do with Ronnie's vigilantes.

The Wall

Chapter 13

When Bugle and Molly arrived at the border they realized they were too late to stop the circus.

The situation was beyond control. The great corporate media conglomerates were heavily vested. Molly saw the rats and remembered stories her mother told her about the old days of rats stealing eggs from nests. She wondered what else they were capable of. When the rabbit family arrived they would be seen as the first phalange of the invasion. They would be wiped out without a chance to explain they were only one family. Molly looked at Bugle. His ears expressed his fear. "I think we better get out of here," he said.

"Can't you see, if we leave the bunnies will be slaughtered by the rats. They look like they mean business. We need to tell them."

"Have you ever tried to reason with a rat?" Bugle asked.

"We can't just leave. Didn't beagles ever hunt rats?"

Bugle could see where this was leading and he didn't like it one bit. "That was generations ago. I am a civilized beagle. I do my hunting at the donut shop."

"Couldn't you pretend?" she asked. "I know you can still bay. You just need to bare your teeth while howling."

Bugle gave a weak growl, curling his lips back to show his cigar-stained teeth. She told him he needed to put more effort into his growl if he was going to be scary. He tried again. Molly could see it was no use. Bugle's bark was gone with his bite. "We'll have to think of a different way," she said.

Bugle felt hurt and decided to give it another try. He stood on his back legs, bared his teeth, and let out a blood curdling howl. Along the fence there was a sudden silence. Little rat heads turned to look, eyes eerily reflecting the stage lights.

"Do it again," she urged, "quickly."

Seeing the rat's reaction, Bugle growled, barked and let out another great howl. Molly looked but it was as if they had seen a mirage. There were no more rats. When the vigilante snakes saw the rats running, they slithered behind, leaving only Ronnie next to the border, alone in his jeep.

Molly turned to look at Bugle, "You've done it," she said with tears in her eyes as she wrapped her wing around his head to give him a hug.

Henry and Tamara heard the howling and knew it must be Bugle and the duck they had met in the desert. They found the rest of the family hiding near the border, having seen the vigilantes. Tamara gave Julie an anti-venom shot and told her family they needed to get to a hospital. The whole family was dehydrated and malnourished. The ten of them, six rabbits, a dog, a duck, a hedgehog, and a tamarin, arrived at the terminal with millions of viewers across the world watching. Lights beat down, blinding them so that Bugle was forced to lead them using his nose which twitched and snorted all the way to the security booth. Once there, Tamara explained that Julie needed immediate medical attention and an ambulance was called to take them both to the hospital. The guard put the rest of them in a waiting room and told them they would have to be interviewed and a security check done before they could enter Animalia.

As this was happening, the door to the checkpoint opened and into the room came a TV camera, followed by lights and a crew of six raccoons, all wearing head phones and carrying microphones. The guard, a handsome 8-point buck, was about to show the new immigrants where to wait when suddenly he was on camera and looking as if he had just been caught in a the headlights of an oncoming car. "You can't bring those in here," he bellowed. Peggy Pigchops stepped through the door and demanded to see the rabbits. "This is Animalia property," the guard replied. He turned to show off his profile, "You need to leave immediately or I will have you arrested."

Peggy told him she was a member of the press and had the right to an interview.

The guard called for backup on his radio and three German shepherds arrived and began unplugging the lights and pushing the cameras out the door. Suddenly they backed away and stood at attention, saluting. The guard looked to see why they had stopped. "What the..." Then he saw and came to attention himself. They all had to focus lower than usual to see the long arthropod that was coming through the door in her full dress uniform, decorations and medals jangling as all one thousand segments made their way into the room. "Can someone please tell me what is going on here? Is the set for "Dancing with the Stars" or a border crossing?"

"I'm here to get the story of the invading rabbits," said Peggy with slightly less authority than usual.

"I see no invasion here," said Millie. "What makes you think there is an invasion happening?"

Peggy explained that everyone knew about it. The Central Animalia press had been talking about it. Marty Moose had sent his deputy, Ronnie Roadkill, to prevent it.

"I suggest you go interview Mr. Roadkill then," said Millie as she ushered Peggy out the door.

Peggy left with her crew in search of Ronnie, and Millie took the rabbits into the waiting room where they told their story. She asked them how the rumor there was a refugee crisis about to land at the entrance to Animalia had gotten started. They were completely in the dark. They had never seen more than a few native bunnies hopping around in the desert, and they all seemed to be doing OK. Each rabbit took a turn explaining his or her own reason for wanting to come to Animalia. Millie began to get it. There was no single reason. The youngsters hoped for a better future than what they could expect back home. The parents hoped it would be easier to feed the family and get medical help for June and Rufus as they needed it. And Rufus and June wanted to be there to see their grandkids grow up. Millie summoned one of the security shepherds and ordered him to give the family a ride to the hospital so they could be with Julie. She took another look for Roadkill. She did not like the fact that a civilian had taken it upon himself to enforce the law. They found him wandering along the fence looking wistfully into the darkness. As she approached, she could hear him talking to himself, "They are coming. I know they are."

"Sir, are you Mr. Ronald Roadkill?" she asked.

He continued to mumble, ignoring her. "Sir, I have to ask you some questions but the answers may be used against you if you are arrested."

"What?"

"Sir, are you the one who was in charge of the volunteers who were at the border earlier this evening?"

"I am a patriot," he said. "I was just going my duty."

"Sir, what you were doing was illegal. You could be prosecuted. Was it your idea to organize the vigilantes to prevent the rabbits from coming into our country?"

Ronnie did not hesitate, "Yes, completely my idea."

Millie could tell he was lying. "You organized and paid for the whole operation? I know candidate Moose was here today. He had nothing to do with this operation?"

90

The Wall

Ronnie said that Mr. Moose was an invited guest to the organizational meeting and had told the group he could not condone any vigilante activity.

She warned him against future efforts and left.

Chapter 14

A week later, Peggy was able to land an interview with Marty Moose at his office. His make-up animals arrived two hours before the cameramen, washed and powdered him to be sure there was no reflections off his shiny coat, and made sure every hair on his main was behaving itself. He had set the terms. He would be in his office, at his desk, and she could sit across from him in the Naugahyde lounge chair. The leather one had been removed. Peggy arrived and sat, checking her notes. She hoped to pin him down on who was responsible for assembling the private police force. She pulled a small mirror from her purse for a last minute check. No food was stuck to her whiskers. Marty came into the room, cashmere sweater draped over his shoulders, collar up on his private label golf shirt, and took a seat behind his formidable desk.

"Hi Peggy," he said.

"Thank you for granting this interview. I know our viewers have been looking forward to hearing what you have to say. So you were at the border when the rabbits arrived and it turned out to be only one family, much to everyone's surprise. What did you think was going to happen?"

"Well, first of all, let me say that I had no preconception of what was going to happen. I only went there because of my concern that it might be something really bad."

Peggy asked, "Do you know this fellow, Mr Roadkill, that was organizing the vigilantes?"

"Of course not," said Marty. "Except that I have heard his name in the news. Let me assure you I have no association with him."

Peggy continued, "Do you believe there will be an invasion of immigrants on our southern border in the near future?"

"I think there is always a threat. Since we are the greatest nation, all animals would love to live here. Why, I have heard that as we sit here, there are thousands of lemmings advancing on the Acadian border to our North."

A year later Peggy found herself back on a flight to Central Animalia City. There had been an amazing scientific discovery, one that was too big to be covered by the science correspondent. A paleontologist, looking for early human remains, had discovered something completely beyond his expertise, but he was sure it was unique. His university, wanting to get credit for the discovery, had alerted the media, so here she was, on a plane, to show the world a completely new species living in the desert. She was told it had a beak like platypus, but instead of a flat tail, it had a round, furry, brown and white one that was constantly in motion, almost like a beagle's.

THE END

Made in the USA
Middletown, DE
17 September 2017